The Wishing Stone

Don't miss any of the chilling adventures!

SPOOKSVILLE

THE WISHING STONE

Christopher Pike

Aladdin

NEW YORK   LONDON   TORONTO   SYDNEY   NEW DELHI

ALADDIN

An imprint of Simon & Schuster Children's Publishing Division
1230 Avenue of the Americas, New York, NY 10020
This Aladdin edition October 2015
Text copyright © 1996 by Christopher Pike
Cover illustration copyright © 2015 by Vivienne To
Also available in an Aladdin paperback edition.
All rights reserved, including the right of reproduction
in whole or in part in any form.
ALADDIN is a trademark of Simon & Schuster, Inc.,
and related logo is a registered trademark of Simon & Schuster, Inc.
For information about special discounts for bulk purchases,
please contact Simon & Schuster Special Sales at 1-866-506-1949
or business@simonandschuster.com.
The Simon & Schuster Speakers Bureau can bring authors to your live event.
For more information or to book an event contact the Simon & Schuster Speakers
Bureau at 1-866-248-3049 or visit our website at www.simonspeakers.com.
Cover designed by Jessica Handelman
Interior designed by Mike Rosamilia
The text of this book was set in Weiss Std.
Manufactured in the United States of America 0915 FFG
2 4 6 8 10 9 7 5 3 1
Library of Congress Control Number 2014946979
ISBN 978-1-4814-1084-7 (hc)
ISBN 978-1-4814-1083-0 (pbk)
ISBN 978-1-4814-1085-4 (eBook)

THE WISHING STONE

1

SALLY WILCOX SAW THE WISHING STONE first. For that reason she felt it belonged mainly to her. That was probably the same reason she suffered more than the others from the stone. The more that was asked of it, the more it demanded in return. Of course no one knew that at first. But even if Sally had known, she probably would have made the same wishes anyway. She was a strong-willed girl, and rather impulsive.

She and her three friends—Cindy Makey, Adam Freeman, and Watch—were not far outside of Spooksville, their hometown, when they first spotted the stone. Since dealing with Pan's leprechauns and fairies in the thick forest high in the hills overlooking the town, they had been staying closer to Spooksville, not wandering too deep into dangerous places that were hard to leave. However, no place in or around Spooksville was really safe. The gang was only hiking in the foothills *of* the foothills when Sally stopped and pointed toward a sparkle in the trees, maybe a quarter of a mile off the path they were taking through a gully.

"What's that?" she asked, brushing aside her dark bangs.

"I don't see anything," Adam, who was shorter than the others, said.

"Neither do I," Watch said, removing his thick glasses and cleaning them on his shirtsleeve. "Did you see an animal?"

"No," Sally said thoughtful. "It was a flash of light."

"It could have just been a reflection," Cindy said, standing behind them.

"Obviously," Sally said, leading the group. "But a reflection of what?" She paused. "I think we should look."

"I don't know," Cindy said, fingering her long blond hair. "If we go off the path, we'll get all dirty."

"And we might run into a strange animal and have our internal organs ripped from our bodies," Watch added.

Sally frowned at Watch. "And you used to be so adventurous," she said.

"I was younger then," Watch said.

"You're only twelve now," Adam observed. He nodded to Sally. "I'll go with you to check it out. It shouldn't take long to hike over there." Sally had pointed to the far side of the gully they were presently hiking through.

"We should probably all go together," Cindy said. "It's not safe to separate out here."

"It's not safe to be alive out here," Sally said.

"But it's better than being dead," Watch said.

They hiked in the direction of the supposed flash Sally had seen. When they reached the spot, they searched the area without seeing anything unusual.

"It was probably just a trick of light," Adam said.

"Perhaps some debris from a crashed flying saucer," Watch added.

But Sally was unconvinced. "It was a bright flash. There must be something strange out here."

"But strange is not necessarily good," Cindy said.

Sally looked at her. "Are you getting scared again?"

"Yes," Cindy said, and added sarcastically, "just being out in the wilderness with you makes me tremble in my shoes."

"Let's continue our hike," said Adam. "Then we can go and get some ice cream."

But Sally was unconvinced. "I want to search the

area one more time. I can do it myself. You guys rest here if you're tired."

In fact, they were all tired. The summer was almost over but obviously the sun didn't know. It was another hot, cloudless day. Adam, Cindy, and Watch plopped down on some boulders in the shade while Sally went off on her own. Cindy had brought a bottle of apple raspberry juice and passed it around.

"Another ten days and school starts," Watch said, taking a deep gulp of the juice and letting out a satisfied sigh. "We won't have many more days like this."

"We'll have the weekends free," Adam, who was new in town, said. "We'll have plenty of time to hang out and have fun."

Watch shook his head as he passed the juice to Adam. "You don't know the teachers in this town. They give you so much homework, you have to work all weekend."

"Why do they do that?" Cindy, who was also new, asked. "We don't all want to grow up to be rocket scientists."

"They just want to give us a chance to complete our studies," Watch said.

"But what's the hurry?" Adam asked.

Watch shrugged. "You've been here long enough to know the answer to that. Not that many kids live long enough to graduate. Last year only about a dozen people graduated from junior high, and half of them were missing body parts."

"What about the other half?" Adam asked reluctantly.

"Most of them were insane," Watch said.

Cindy grimaced. "That's horrible!"

"I don't know," Watch said. "They had a great all-night graduation party."

"I hope we get to be in a lot of classes together," Adam said.

Watch shook his head. "It might be better to separate. Then, if there is an explosion or something, at least one of us will survive."

"You have explosions at school?" Cindy asked. "I don't believe it."

"We had a half-dozen explosions last year. Most of them were in chemistry class. The teacher used to work for the CIA." Watch added, "But I think they got rid of him."

Suddenly they heard Sally shouting.

"I've found something! I've found something!"

2

Sally had indeed found something, an extraordinary something. Sitting atop a granite boulder nestled between two thick trees was a perfectly sculpted black hand. It rose right out of the rock, its palm pointed toward the sky. The fingers were not completely open, but were clenched around a cube-shaped crystal stone. The stone was as large as a normal man's hand could comfortably hold, at most two inches on a side. Although the nearby trees were close together, sunlight occasionally pierced through the branches to land on the stone. When this happened there was a bright flash. The stone was clear but it also acted like a mirror, which puzzled Adam.

Now they knew what had caught Sally's eye.

"Isn't it beautiful?" Sally asked, excited.

"Yes," Cindy said. "But what is it?"

Adam nodded seriously. "Good question. And where did it come from I wonder." He paused. "Have you touched it, Sally?"

"No. I was waiting for you guys."

"We might want to leave it alone," Watch suggested. "We don't know who it belongs to."

"It belongs to me," Sally said. "I found it."

"And does every bike you pass on the street belong to you?" Cindy asked. "Every skateboard? Just because you find something doesn't mean it's yours."

"It does if you find it in the middle of nowhere," Sally said, reaching out to pick up the crystal. Adam stopped her.

"Watch is right," he said. "We have to be careful."

Sally was impatient. "All right, say we take the safe course and talk about this for the next hour. In the end we all know none of us is going to leave this stone here for someone else to find. It's too pretty. I say we take it now and be done with it."

"Hold on." Adam peered at the black hand, trying to figure out what it was made of. It seemed to be some type of shiny metal, yet when he touched it the hand felt warm. He told the others as much.

7

"Could it be alive?" Cindy whispered.

"It's black," Watch said. "If the sun was shining on it that might have made it hot."

Adam studied the thick overhead trees. "I don't think the sun made it warm."

"I don't care about the hand," Sally said. "I'm only interested in the crystal." Again she reached out to take it. "Don't stop me, Adam."

None of them stopped her this time, and a second later she was holding the clear cube, rubbing it with her fingers, savoring it as if it were a diamond.

"Maybe it's a diamond," Sally said. "Maybe I can sell it for ten million dollars."

"Naturally you would share the profits with us, your best friends," Cindy said.

Sally snorted. "You guys wanted to leave it here. And now that I'm holding it and you can see it's safe, you want to make money from it."

"We reserve judgment as to how safe it is," Watch said.

"I'm more concerned with who it belongs to," Adam said. "I really wish you wouldn't take it, Sally."

She remained stubborn. "If anyone reports it missing I'll return it immediately." She held it up to the sunlight and the crystal sparkled, sending out tiny shafts of light through all the trees. "Until then it is mine."

"Look!" Cindy cried. "The black hand closed!"

Cindy was right. The hand that had once held the crystal was now entirely shut. Apparently the fingers had closed while they were talking.

"It is alive," Cindy gasped. "Quick, Sally, put the crystal back."

Sally hesitated. "Just because it moved doesn't mean it's alive."

"I don't see many of these rocks getting up and doing a dance," Watch said.

Adam spoke seriously. "It doesn't belong to you, Sally. Taking it is stealing."

Sally considered. "All right, I'll put it back." She held it close to the black hand, thinking the hand would grab it. When that didn't happen Sally tried to push it in between the bent fingers. But the hand was clenched tight. Finally she gave up. "It doesn't want it."

"Then just leave it beside the hand," Adam suggested. "It can reach over and grab the stone later, if it wants."

"No," Sally said. "I don't think that's fair. If the hand wants it, it should take it now."

"I doubt that a disembodied black hand understands our concept of fairness," Watch said.

"I'm not just going to leave it here," Sally said.

"Thief," Cindy muttered.

"Coward!" Sally snapped at her.

Adam held up his hands. "Hold on, let's not have another fight. Maybe we can work out a compromise."

"There's no compromise," Sally said. "I either take it or I don't."

"You could leave a note with your home address on it," Cindy said. "That way if the black hand wants the stone back it can crawl to your house in the middle of the night, choke you to death, and take it home."

"A novel suggestion," Watch said.

"We can argue about this all day," Adam said, resigned to Sally's ways. "If you're going to take it, then take it, and let's get out of here."

"But please walk at least fifty feet behind us," Cindy said.

"I always walk a hundred feet in front of you." Sally clasped the crystal to her chest. "I'm not afraid to go where no woman has gone before."

They hiked back toward the path. Along the way Sally stubbed her toe and let out a groan. "I wish I had a new pair of shoes," she said, letting them pass her on the path. "These are getting so short and worn out—they hurt my feet."

Without warning, Sally let out a scream.

They turned anxiously. Sally was so stunned she

couldn't speak. She could only point. It took them a moment to register what her scream was all about. Then it struck them and they let out their own individual sounds of amazement.

There were brand-new shoes on Sally's feet.

3

IT MUST BE A WISHING STONE," WATCH said after they had all had a chance to catch their breath. "Bum has spoken about them before."

"He has?" Sally asked, amazed once again by how much Bum knew. Bum was just that—the town bum. A bum who had once been the town mayor.

Watch continued, "Bum said they could be found on Earth during the Atlantis and Lemuria ages, tens of thousands of years ago. You remember, he said that Spooksville was actually once a part of Lemuria. In fact, he says that Spooksville is all that is left of Lemuria."

"Did the people at that time make these Wishing Stones?" Adam asked.

Watch was thoughtful. "Bum didn't go into too much detail. But I got the impression the stones were put here by extraterrestrial visitors."

"You mean aliens?" Cindy asked.

"Not necessarily," Watch said. "Bum believes this planet was originally colonized by humans from other planets."

"He mentioned the Pleiades star cluster before," Adam said. "Did the Wishing Stones come from there?"

Watch was uncertain. "He never said one way or the other. But I got the impression they were from someplace even farther away."

"Did he say the stones were dangerous?" Cindy asked.

"He laughed when he talked about them, as he usually does when he talks about anything really mysterious," Watch said. "I was never sure if they were dangerous or not. But I do know that whoever holds one can ask for whatever he or she wants, and it will instantly appear." He nodded to Sally's new sneakers. "But we know that already."

"Can I get as many wishes as I want?" Sally asked.

"I don't think the stones ever run out of power," Watch said.

Sally squealed with delight. "Wow! This is absolutely

awesome. I'm going to have everything I ever wanted before I turn thirteen."

"You can get us some things, too," Cindy said.

Sally laughed at her. "*Now* you change your mind. *Now* you think I did the right thing."

Cindy was indignant. "I just don't think you should be greedy, that's all."

Sally patted her on the back. "Don't worry, girl, you can have what you want. All I ask is that you act nice to me."

Watch turned to Adam. "I think the three of us had better not expect anything."

Sally smiled. "That's not true; I can grant you guys some wishes. But first I want to get a few things for myself." She gestured for them to stand back. "I don't want you crowding my presents."

"Wait!" Adam said. "We don't know what these wishes might cost."

Sally stared at him as if he were nuts. "Why should they cost me anything? This is a Wishing Stone. It's not a bill collector."

"But you don't get anything for free in this world," Adam said.

"But," Sally countered, "this stone, Watch says, did not come from this world."

"She has a point there," Watch said.

Adam was still worried. "I think you should be happy with your new shoes and leave it at that."

Sally laughed again. "You have to start thinking big, Mr. Adam Freeman. You don't accept getting a lousy pair of shoes when you have the whole world available. Now quiet down and let me think what I want."

"You should get some new clothes," Cindy suggested.

"Maybe a new watch," Watch, who always wore four watches, said.

"Shh," Sally said, closing her eyes and letting her smile grow larger. "I have something. Yes, this is what I want." She paused and then blurted out the next words. "I wish I had a million dollars!"

A million dollars suddenly appeared.

Hundreds of stacks of one-dollar bills, which literally stood in piles above their heads. Adam could hardly believe his eyes. Reaching out, he grabbed one of the stacks and studied it. The bills appeared genuine. Sally squealed again with joy.

"I'm rich!" she said.

"You should have asked for hundred-dollar denominations," Watch said. "You're never going to be able to get all this stuff back to your house."

"Even if you could," Cindy said, "you couldn't fit it in your house."

Sally snickered. "You guys are just jealous! I'm a millionaire and you're not."

"Well, maybe you could give us all loans," Watch said.

"I want some new clothes," Cindy said suddenly.

"Wait a second," Adam said. But no one was listening.

"What do you want?" Sally asked Cindy.

Cindy rubbed her hands together. "I'd love a black leather jacket and some black leather boots. Then I need some clothes for school. How about a Gap sweater and skirt? Light yellow to match my hair."

"You need this to go to school in Spooksville?" Watch asked.

Sally waved her hand. "It doesn't matter. If she wants it she wants it." Sally closed her eyes, then spoke out loud and wished for what Cindy had just requested.

The clothes did not appear.

Sally opened her eyes and studied the stone. "It can't be worn out already. Watch?"

"It's possible Cindy has to make her own wishes," he said. "You don't really want these clothes, not the way you wanted the million dollars. Give Cindy the stone and we'll see."

"I'm not giving her the stone," Sally said quickly.

"I'll give it back," Cindy said.

"How do I know you will?" Sally asked suspiciously.

Cindy was insulted. "When have I ever stolen any-thing of yours?"

"When have I ever had a Wishing Stone before?" Sally asked.

"This is getting ridiculous," Adam interrupted. "The stone is already causing problems. Let's put it back."

"There are a couple of things I would like," Watch said.

Adam was stunned. "But I thought you agreed with me?"

Watch smiled. "I did until I saw the million dollars."

"I'll give Watch the stone first," Sally said. "As an experiment."

"What's wrong with me?" Cindy complained.

"Nothing's wrong with you," Sally said impatiently. "But I've known Watch longer than you. I know for a fact he'll give the stone back when I ask for it." She went to hand the stone to Watch and then stopped. "You will give it back to me, won't you?"

Watch shrugged. "Sure."

"Swear on your life," Sally ordered.

"It's not good to swear," Cindy said.

"I swear to whatever you want me to swear to," Watch said.

"All right." Sally reluctantly handed over the stone. "Don't break it."

Watch held the stone close to his heart and closed his eyes. For a moment he concentrated deeply. Then he spoke. "I wish for a six-inch refractor telescope with clock drive and computer-assisted star finder."

The telescope appeared just off the path.

"Cool," Watch said.

"Let me try!" Cindy exclaimed.

"It's my turn," Sally snapped. "Watch, give me the stone back."

"Just a moment," Watch said, closing his eyes once more. "I wish for a laser pistol."

A black pistol-shaped device materialized at his feet.

Watch knelt and picked it up. He pointed it at a nearby rock and pulled the trigger. There was a flash of red light. The rock exploded into a thousand pieces. The gang jumped, except for Watch. He studied the weapon closer.

"It's interesting," he muttered.

"It's very powerful," Adam gasped.

"What I mean," Watch continued, "is that the Wishing Stone was able to materialize something that doesn't even exist on this planet. That's proof that it must be from another world."

"I'm waiting," Sally said with her hand outstretched.

"Just a second," Watch said, closing his eyes once

more. "I wish for the finest portal power shield generator in the entire galaxy."

A small black, oval-shaped object appeared at his feet.

Watch knelt and picked this up as well. There were a series of buttons on the side and he experimented with them for a moment. Then he handed the laser pistol to Adam.

"I want you to shoot me," he said.

Adam shook his head. "No way. Do you think that force field generator will protect you? What if it doesn't? You'll die."

"I have set the laser pistol on stun," Watch said.

"How do you know for sure?" Adam asked.

"Shoot Sally and see if it knocks her out," Watch said.

Sally jumped back and held out her hands. "Don't shoot me! Shoot Cindy!"

Cindy didn't look too happy about that suggestion. "Don't shoot anybody!" she shouted.

"Shoot a tree then," Watch said. "It really is set to stun."

"You can't stun a tree," Sally said. "They're permanently stunned."

Nevertheless, Adam turned and shot the nearest tree. Once again a red beam of light struck out, yet it left no noticeable impression on the tree bark. Adam decided it was safe enough to fire at his friend.

"You sure you have the force field on?" he asked Watch, taking aim.

"Pretty sure," Watch said. "The force field must be invisible. But the worst that can happen is I'll be knocked out."

"Give me the Wishing Stone first," Sally said, moving to retrieve the stone from him. But as she neared him it was as if she smashed into an invisible wall. She bounced back in midstride. Adam and Cindy laughed.

"The force field is definitely working," Cindy said. "Watch, you should leave it on all the time."

"That way Sally will never get the stone back," Adam added.

"Don't worry," Watch reassured Sally. "You'll have it back in a second. But stand back right now. Adam, fire away."

Adam once more took aim with the laser pistol and fired. The red beam sprayed over a point two feet from Watch's body, but it didn't touch him. Adam ceased firing and Watch turned off the force field. Adam handed the laser back to his friend. Watch admired the two instruments.

"I've always wanted gadgets like this," Watch said.

Adam was happy for him even though he continued to be afraid of the Wishing Stone. "I'm sure they'll come in handy living in this town," Adam said. "Especially if the Cold People or the demons come back."

"Thank you very much," Sally said, snatching the Wishing Stone from Watch's hands. "You already have more than I do, and I'm the one who found it. Stand back, all of you. It's Christmas time in Spooksville."

"But what about my new clothes?" Cindy asked.

"You'll get those when I'm through," Sally said.

She then proceeded to order new clothes for herself: a new bedroom set, a new TV and CD player, and another million dollars—in hundred-dollar bills. When Cindy finally got her hands on the Wishing Stone she didn't hold back, either: more clothes, a new bike, hundreds of CD's, boxes of books, and every known computer game. Soon the path was littered with so much stuff it would have taken several large moving vans to haul it all away.

Adam said as much. "Most of this is just going to go to waste out here. You should have made your wishes back in town."

"We can bring the stuff back piece by piece," Sally said, stuffing her pockets with hundred-dollar bills. "That reminds me, Adam. What do you want?"

Adam shook his head. "Nothing."

Sally held out the Wishing Stone. "Come on, don't be a moralist. At least get yourself some new clothes. You look like your mother dresses you."

Adam was insulted. "My mother does buy all my clothes."

"There you go," Cindy said, trying on a sweater over her T-shirt.

Adam was even more insulted. "You really think I dress like a nerd?"

"I didn't say the nerd word," Cindy said quickly.

"But she was obviously thinking it," Sally said, still holding the stone out to him to take. "Improve your image, Adam, what can it hurt?"

"You might want to get yourself a laser pistol," Watch said. "We could play war games together."

Adam reluctantly accepted the Wishing Stone. "I'm not going to wish for anything for myself," he said.

"But it only works if you really want what you're wishing for," Cindy said.

"I can really want something and it doesn't have to be only for myself," Adam said. Holding the Wishing Stone tight, he closed his eyes and said with as much feeling as possible, "I wish for galactic peace!"

Nothing happened, of course. Nothing that they

could see. The others stared at him as if he had lost his mind.

"What good is a wish like that?" Sally asked.

Adam shrugged. "It's something I'd like. For every-body to live in peace."

"Wasn't world peace big enough for you?" Watch asked.

"We've been talking about people on other planets," Adam said. "Why should I leave them out?"

"But get something for yourself," Cindy said. "A new skateboard at least."

"Yeah," Watch said. "You're making the rest of us feel guilty."

Adam handed the Wishing Stone back to Sally. "Maybe later," he said. "I don't need anything right now."

For the time being that settled that discussion. They spent the next ten minutes trying to figure out how much they could carry back to town. Even though it was a warm day, Cindy had gone behind a bush and dressed herself in *two* new outfits at once. Sally was mainly preoccupied with carrying away as much cash as possible. And Watch quickly discovered he couldn't move his telescope very far, and ended up taking only the laser pistol and the portal force field generator with him. Adam helped Cindy with her new bike.

"Next I'm going to wish for a gold credit card," Sally said as she skipped in front of them with the Wishing Stone in her hand.

4

THEY WERE TEN MINUTES ON THEIR WAY
when a man in a red, hooded robe appeared on the path
in front of them. The shadow cast by the hood obscured
his face, making it a black well of mystery. But in the
shadow two eyes glittered out at them with a wicked red
light. The man was tall with exceptionally long arms.
He raised a hand as they stood stock-still, stunned by
his sudden appearance. It was only then that Sally and
the others realized his hands were identical to the one
they had found sticking up from the granite boulder
where the Wishing Stone had been.

"I am the Collector," he said in a strangely mechanical voice. "I am here to collect on your debt."

"I was worried something like this would happen," Adam muttered.

"This character surpasses the worst fear I had," Sally whispered, her voice shaking. "What are we going to do?"

"Maybe you could give him some of your cash," Cindy said anxiously.

"I don't think this guy can be bought off," Watch said.

"Let me try talking to him," Adam said, hesitantly taking a step forward. He waved to the figure and cleared his throat. "Hi, my name's Adam Freeman and these are my friends. What exactly is this debt you're talking about?"

The cloaked figure lowered his right hand and a metallic scroll mysteriously appeared in it. He read from it in his peculiar computer-animated voice. It didn't sound as if he were living, but rather something built in an alien laboratory.

"Sara Wilcox—ten thousand and sixty-four gratoms," he said. "Cindy Makey—one thousand and eighty-two gratoms. Watch—With No Known Last Name—nine hundred and forty-one gratoms. Adam Freeman—you owe . . ." The dark figure's speech trailed off. "Your debt has yet to be totaled, but it looks as if it will be large." He paused. "These were all placed on the same order."

"This is from the stuff we wished for with the Wishing Stone?" Adam asked.

"Yes. The debt is due immediately and must be paid in full."

"We didn't know that," Adam said.

"It does not matter. I am the Collector. I am here to collect your debts. Now."

"Ask if we can just give the stuff back," Cindy suggested.

"Maybe not all of it," Sally muttered.

"Can we pay off the debt by returning the goods?" Adam asked.

"There is a no-refund policy. Your debts are due immediately. Hand over the gratoms now."

"But we don't have any gratoms," Watch said. "We don't even know what they are."

The Collector moved his fingers and the metallic scroll vanished. In its place was a small spherical-shaped object lined with numerous glowing buttons and flashing lights. It hummed as it sat in the Collector's hand, filling each of them with an ominous feeling.

"The debt must be paid immediately," the Collector said in his robotic voice. "If you cannot pay, then you must work off the debt on a slave planet."

Adam held up a hand. "Now wait a second. This isn't

fair. This Wishing Stone was just sitting in the middle of nowhere. No instructions came with it. There wasn't even a warning label on the side. We can't be responsible for debts we had no idea we were piling up."

"I am a Collector," the hooded figure repeated. "I am here to collect your debts. I do not argue over how you accumulated these debts. And since you have made it clear that you have no gratoms to pay for these debts, you will now be transported to a slave planet where you will spend the rest of your lives working off these debts." He fiddled with the controls on the sphere in his hands. "Stand ready to be transported to Amacron Thirty-seven."

"Wait!" Adam pleaded. "We're not ready to be transported anywhere. We need to talk about this some more."

"We should at least be allowed to talk to a lawyer," Sally said, stepping forward and angrily pointing a finger at the Collector. "You show up here, saying you're a Collector and we're supposed to pay you. How do we know you're not a fake? You haven't even shown us ID. You haven't even—" Sally was cut off in midsentence.

There was a flash of green light. It came from the sphere.

And Sally was gone. Just gone.

"Oh no," Cindy cried.

There was another flash of green light.

Then Cindy was gone.

"Get out of the way, Adam!" Watch shouted.

Adam wasn't even given a chance to think. He dove to the side of the path. This time there was a burst of red light. Adam felt sure he was on his way to some forsaken slave world. But then the Collector collapsed on the path and the transporting sphere rolled lazily into the bushes. Out the corner of his eye Adam saw Watch lowering his laser pistol.

"I wish I was a faster draw," Watch said.

Adam understood. They had lost the girls. Adam stood and brushed off his pants. Together they stepped to where the Collector had fallen. He lay facedown covered by his hood. Watch reached down to feel for a pulse at the guy's neck, then he jerked his hand back.

"I think I killed him," he whispered. "But, I promise, the laser was set to stun."

Adam shook his hand. "I don't think this guy was ever alive. You heard his voice. He's got to be a robot."

Watch stood and nodded grimly. "You're probably right. Maybe the stun was enough to destroy his positronic brain." He pointed to the sphere that had rolled into the bushes. "I wonder if we can figure how to use that."

Adam stepped over and picked it up. Although it was small, there were at least twenty controls on the object. "It would take a genius to understand how to operate it."

"I'm supposed to have a genius IQ," Watch said. "Give it to me."

Adam handed it over. "What is your IQ?"

"One hundred and sixty."

"I'm impressed."

"I try not to brag about it," Watch said.

While Watch was examining the device, Adam studied the spots where Cindy and Sally had disappeared. There were no burn marks on the ground, nothing to show that they had been beamed away to another planet. Amacron 37—it sounded awfully far from home to Adam. He was about to turn back to Watch when a flash of light in the grass nearby caught his eye.

Sally had dropped the Wishing Stone.

Adam brought it over to Watch. "It must have fallen from her hand during the transportation process," Adam said.

"We might want to order up a few more laser pistols before the Collector's pals come looking for him," Watch said.

"I think that would just bring his pals quicker." Adam gestured to the fallen Collector, who had yet to move an inch. "I don't think we have all that much time. Have you been able to figure out how it works?"

"I know how to turn it on. I watched what the Collector did when he zapped Sally and Cindy. But that isn't the same as knowing how to operate it."

"Maybe we don't have to know everything. The settings should be the same as when the Collector zapped the girls. If we zap ourselves, we should go to the same place."

Watch was doubtful. "Maybe."

"We have to give it a try."

Watch hesitated. "Do we want to do that? I mean, that slave labor planet didn't sound like a vacation spot."

"We have no choice. If we don't save the girls, who will?"

"If we can't save the girls, then who'll save us?"

Adam was astounded. "I can't believe you'd leave the girls to suffer lives of torment and misery."

"I didn't say that was my first choice. I was just reviewing all our options."

"What other options do we have?" Adam asked.

"We could go home and pretend none of this ever happened." Watch stopped and scratched his head. "But I don't suppose we'd be able to live with that decision." He gestured Adam closer. "Get right beside me. I'll try to zap us both at the same time. That might increase the odds that we go to the same place."

Adam pressed up against Watch and stared at the mysterious sphere, which Watch held out at arm's length. "What if it beams us into deep space?" he asked.

"Then we'll have a hard time catching our breath."

"Should we bring the Wishing Stone with us?"

"Yes," Watch said, his finger on a purple button. "We might be wishing for a couple of space suits in the next ten seconds."

"I knew you were going to say that," Adam replied, stuffing the stone in his pocket.

Watch pushed the button and the Earth vanished.

5

AMACRON 37 WAS DESOLATE AND MISER-
able, a desert planet with two yellow moons and a
purple sun. The wind blew thin and dry fifteen hours
a day, which was the length of Amacron 37's day. Yet
the air was not particularly hot—just unsatisfying. The
world was obviously old and burnt out, with barely
enough oxygen to support life. When Sally and Cindy
first materialized on the planet, they wondered if they'd
survive the night.

There had been no transition for them. One minute they were on the path with Adam and Watch—and
the Collector—and the next they were being herded
toward a desolate barracks by a couple of robots with

electric prods. When the prods touched the girls, they were given sharp jolts. They neither argued with the robots nor put up a fight, although Sally got shocked once just for stumbling in the sand. The voltage wasn't excessively high but it did hurt. But basically they were too confused to do much of anything except what they were told.

The inside of the barracks was dusty and dark. They were shown to a couple of hard mats and told to rest until their shift began. Apparently they had been transported at the end of the work day. The tiny purple sun was still in the sky, along with the two tired moons. Glancing around the dim barracks, they could see that not all the inhabitants were humanoid. There were a couple of huge bearlike creatures and one guy who was a cross between a spider and an overgrown butterfly. Yet they all seemed to be resting as no one stood to greet them.

One of the robots gestured with its electric stick. "You will be called to labor in five zomas," it said.

"How long is a zoma in human hours?" Sally asked.

"Forty minutes," the robot said, and turned away with his companion, leaving them alone.

Sally and Cindy sat on their respective bunks. They had left home only minutes ago but already they had sand in their ears from the short walk outside. Both looked as miserable as they felt.

"I wonder where the guys are?" Sally said finally.

"Maybe they were transported to another planet," Cindy said.

"The Collector implied that we were all going to Amacron Thirty-seven." Sally paused. "Maybe they escaped somehow."

"I doubt it. They were probably just transported to another part of this planet."

Sally was thoughtful. "Watch had the laser pistol. Maybe he blew the Collector away."

"Even if he did, I don't think that's going to help us."

Sally sighed. "All that good stuff isn't any use here."

Cindy agreed. "You'd think they'd have let us bring it with us. It looks like we'll be paying for it for a long time."

A soft voice spoke near them. "You only get what you wished for after you pay off your debts."

They looked over at the neighboring bunk. A girl who appeared to be about their age, with a green face and white eyes, sat up and studied them. Her hair was long and black, so tightly curled that it would have been longer than she was tall if it were straightened out. She was beautiful, even with a green face, even by human standards. Plus her voice was a thing of music, gentle and melodious.

"Who are you?" Sally asked.

"My name is Hironee. What are your names?"

"I'm Sally and this is Cindy." Sally paused. "Have you been here long?"

Hironee was grave. "Half my life. I assume you are from Earth?"

"Yeah," Cindy said. "You've heard of the place?"

"I had a friend who was from there. His name was Charles. He taught me your language. Except for the local boss and the robots—who know every language in the galaxy—I am the only one on Amacron Thirty-seven who knows English."

"But what happened to Charles?" Cindy asked.

Hironee spoke sadly. "He was here for five years and then one day he couldn't take it anymore and tried to escape." Hironee lowered her head. "The robots caught him in the desert and burned him to a crisp."

"Has anyone ever escaped from here?" Sally asked.

Hironee glanced up. "There are stories that a few have escaped, over the last ten thousand years. But no one has done it while I've been here. This particular camp is surrounded by an invisible force field. To get out into the deep desert, you have to disable the force field, which Charles did by making a bomb out of chemicals in the soil. But then there is nowhere to go in the desert. Either the elements kill you or the robots find you and cut you down with their lasers."

"What planet are you from?" Cindy asked.

Hironee brightened. "My planet is named Zanath. It is very beautiful, littered with what you would call tropical islands. I was very happy there." She added wistfully, "I miss it very much."

"Were you brought here by a Collector?" Sally asked.

"Yes. I accidentally found a Wishing Stone and made a few wishes before the Collector appeared and demanded I pay him five hundred and sixteen gratoms."

"Exactly how long have you been here?" Sally asked.

"Four of your years."

"How many gratoms have you worked off in that time?"

"Three gratoms," Hironee said, and laughed softly, a sad, low laugh. "It really doesn't matter what your debt is. You will never pay it off before you die. That's the way the Kasters set up the system."

"That's what I suspected," Sally said grimly.

"Who are the Kasters?" Cindy asked.

"They are the ones who construct the Wishing Stones. They seed them on planets all over the galaxy and use them to ensnare slave labor. The more advanced civilizations are aware of them and never use the stones. But the Kasters are always finding fresh slaves to work for them. They are shady businessmen, a greedy race of reptiles with a ruthless reputation for cheating and extortion. They also construct the robots who run this slave planet and many others like it."

"Are there any Kasters here?" Sally asked.

"One. His name is Teeh, and he is horrible. He is the one I told you about who also speaks English. You'll meet him tomorrow—he goes out of his way to harass new slaves." Hironee lowered her voice. "Don't ever anger him. He'll peel the skin off your body and eat it in front of you. I've seen him do it."

"Why don't the more advanced civilizations in the galaxy stop the Kasters from taking slaves?" Cindy asked.

"The Kasters are a powerful and feared race. They take only slaves from those who have become indebted to them. This is what you would call a loophole in the galactic law. It allows them to operate just outside the law. Plus a lot of races still buy Kaster goods. There is always a market for them. Here on this planet you will make Kaster lamps for the rest of your lives." Hironee shrugged. "They're pretty good lamps. They'll last longer than we will."

"We will not remain here for the rest of our lives," Sally said flatly. "We are going to escape. I don't care how long it takes, but we will not stay here and make lamps for a bunch of slimy reptiles."

Hironee cautioned Sally to lower her voice. She glanced around the barracks, her white eyes glittering in the dark.

"Be careful what you say. Teeh has spies everywhere. We can talk about such matters during the work shift when not so many ears are close. But I can tell you now it is better, in the long run, to accept your situation and try to live with it. There is no real chance of escape. Remember what happened to Charles."

Sally lowered her voice to a whisper. "Cindy and I are from Spooksville. It's the roughest town on Earth. You may have heard about it from Charles. It's prepared us for places like this. I don't want to brag about our past but let's just say we've been in worse fixes than this before."

"We have?" Cindy asked.

Sally continued as if she hadn't heard her. "Cindy and I are intelligent and resourceful. We will never accept this situation." Sally glanced out the barracks window at the setting purple sun. "The Kasters are going to regret they ever brought us here."

6

ADAM AND WATCH MATERIALIZED UNDER-
ground in a huge rocky cavern. The place was far from
empty but their sudden appearance didn't even cause a
stir. There had to be a hundred different races milling
about the cavern, which seemed to be a marketplace of
sorts. There were creatures of every color and shape—
some looked more like monsters than intelligent beings,
especially the insectile beings. Adam shuddered as a
couple came close and stared at him with several hundred emotionless eyes.

"Those two look like they'd like to have us for din-
ner," Adam muttered.

"Yeah," Watch said. "I think we'd better get off this

platform. It's probably where people beam into this place."

They headed into a corner of the cavern, in the direction of what looked like a food place. There were numerous tables set up and people were feasting on exotic dishes. Between the tables squat robots with square heads took orders and delivered meals.

"Do you think this is Amacron Thirty-seven?" Adam asked.

"No," Watch said without hesitating. "This is not a slave planet. All these people look like they're out for an afternoon of shopping."

"But why would the transporter send us to another planet?"

"You forget the Collector dropped the sphere as he fell," Watch explained, still holding the instrument in his right hand. The laser he had tucked in his belt, under his shirt. "A button was probably pushed that moved the destination control to the next place on the list."

"Makes sense. But maybe someone here can tell us how to set the sphere for the slave planet."

"We might want to find out about Amacron Thirty-seven before we go barging in," Watch said, finally putting the sphere in his front pocket.

Adam nodded. "Good idea." He pointed to the far corner. "Let's sit at that table and act like we belong."

They weren't seated long before one of the square-headed robots approached them to take their orders. It looked like a box of metal on wheels, except for its mouth, which faintly resembled a human mouth with a serious case of braces. It nodded as it approached and then gestured with an aluminum arm for them to speak, probably to figure out what planet they were from and what language they used. They figured this had to be correct because right after Adam and Watch said hello, it replied in a clear mechanical voice:

"Earth. English."

"That's correct," Watch said. "You speak English?"

"Fluently. What would you two sentient beings like to eat and drink?"

Adam glanced at Watch. "We don't have any gratoms. We better not order anything."

"There is no charge for these services," the robot interrupted. "What would you like to eat and drink?"

Watch removed his glasses and cleaned them on the tail of his shirt. "What do you have?" he asked.

"To repeat verbally our complete menu in the English language would take a long time," the robot said. "But we do have a wide variety of Earth dishes.

Perhaps you could order and I will tell you if we can meet your needs."

Adam brightened. "Could I have a turkey sandwich on white toast, with lettuce and tomato, no mayonnaise? And an order of French fries and a large Coke?"

"Certainly," the robot said. He turned to Watch. "And you, sir?"

"I would like a pepperoni pizza with a large Coke."

"Is that all?"

"Bring us some chocolate-chip cookies as well," Watch said.

The robot was agreeable. "Your order will take ten earth minutes to prepare. But I can bring your drinks within two minutes." The robot turned to leave.

"Excuse me," Adam said. "Just before you go. What planet is this?"

"This is not a planet, sir, but an asteroid. Its name is Globar Ninety-two."

"Are we far from Amacron Thirty-seven?" Watch asked.

"Yes. Two thousand seven hundred and eighteen point six light-years."

"Thank you," Adam said. "My friend and I will have ice with our Cokes."

The robot left and Watch nodded seriously. "I

suspected we were on an asteroid. Notice that this whole place is underground?"

"Yeah. But at least it's nice that we don't have to pay for lunch."

"We should wait until we get our food to see how nice it is."

Watch's concern proved groundless. The food—when it arrived—was very good. The Cokes, in fact, tasted identical to Earth's, but the robot explained that they were popular in even this part of the galaxy. Adam practically wolfed down his sandwich. Fighting with mysterious forces always made him hungry.

It was while they were eating their cookies that the stranger arrived. One moment they were alone and the next he was standing beside their table.

"May I join you?" he asked. But those were not exactly the words that came from his mouth. He spoke another language, but a voice box clipped to his belt provided them with the translation. Indeed, he had two extra boxes with him, which he quickly offered to Adam and Watch. Apparently they were universal translators that were often employed in such places as Globar 92. Adam and Watch clipped them onto their own belts.

"Sure," Adam said as the box translated his word into the visitor's language. "You can sit down."

"But before you do, we would prefer you to tell us what you want," Watch said.

Adam understood Watch's concern. The guy would have stood out at a Halloween party. He was ghastly thin and white as a bed sheet. His features were human as far as shape and function, but his eyes were completely blue, as was his long robe. To top it off he was smoking a fat cigar and didn't have a trace of hair on his body. On the crown of his head he wore a square blue cap. He blew cigar smoke Watch's way as Watch's comment was translated by the box he had just clipped to his belt.

"My name is Fur," he said. "I am well known in these parts. Ask anybody about me, they'll give you a good recommendation."

"What would they recommend you for?" Adam asked.

"I am a trader," Fur said. "I make deals, good deals. May I sit down?"

"Yes," Adam said. "I'm Adam and this is Watch."

"Pleased to meet you both."

"Why are you called Fur?" Watch asked. "You look like you don't have a hair on your body."

Fur appeared displeased as he pulled up a chair. "Is it the custom on your world to insult somebody because he is bald?" He stroked his shiny white head. "When I get a little ahead, I plan on having a hair transplant."

"Where are they going to transplant it from?" Watch asked. "Your twin sister?"

"Fur," Adam said quickly. "My friend doesn't mean to be rude. We're just curious about what you want." He added, "We're strangers here."

"I can see that," Fur said. "I spotted you the moment you came in, and have been studying you since." He paused. "I know you're from Earth, and that you're young by that society's standards."

"We're not that young," Watch said.

Fur smiled and they saw that his teeth were blue as well. "I am not bald and you are not young. Very well, we are off to a good start." He leaned closer and lowered his voice. The translator softened as well—it was clearly capable of distinguishing different emotional tones. "I couldn't help noticing that you came in carrying a Kaster transporter."

"We did?" Adam asked. "I mean, yeah, so what? It's a good make."

Fur's smile broadened. "The Kasters do not sell their transporters, not willingly. I can only assume you obtained this one through—how should I put it?—unusual means."

Watch shrugged. "I don't see what business that is of yours."

Fur shrugged. "I am not interested in how you got it. I just want to know if you want to sell it."

"No," Watch said.

"Don't you want to know what I would give you for it in return?" Fur asked.

"No," Watch said.

Adam raised a hand. "Just a second, Watch. Let's listen and see what's available." He paused. "What are you offering, Mr. Fur?"

"Just call me Fur. I can offer you pretty much whatever you want." He laughed out loud. "You really should ask about me. They'll tell you that there's nothing Fur can't get you, and quick."

"Except perhaps a Kaster transporter," Watch said.

Fur lost his smile. "They are not easily available, it is true. But come, name your price. I am willing to bargain."

"Can you give us twenty thousand gratoms?" Watch asked.

Fur blinked. "You can't be serious? I don't have that kind of wealth. There isn't a sentient being in this place who does. What's the matter? Do you owe a Kaster Collector a Wishing Stone debt?"

Adam hesitated. "As a matter of fact we do."

Fur nodded, taking it all in. "And the Collector appeared and tried to collect the debt. And somehow you two destroyed the Collector and took its transporter. I see the whole picture now. Am I right?"

"You're close," Adam admitted. "Before we could take care of the Collector, it managed to transport two of our friends to Amacron Thirty-seven." He added, "They're Sally and Cindy. I don't suppose you've heard about them?"

Fur was grave. "I have not heard of them nor will they ever be heard from again. If they have gone to a Kaster slave planet, there is no escape for them. They are doomed to work as slaves for the remainder of their lives."

"Sally always was a good worker," Watch said, trying to put a positive spin on the matter. But Adam was appalled.

"There must be some way to save them," he said.

Fur shook his head. Apparently that meant no in that part of the galaxy, too.

"The Kasters keep perfect records," he explained. "They never allow a debt to go unpaid. That is the cornerstone of their ruthless reputation. Even if you could somehow get onto Amacron Thirty-seven—

which would be next to impossible—they would still have a record of your friends' debts. They would hunt them down to the last corner of the galaxy and make them pay."

"Where are these records kept?" Watch asked.

Fur had to think. "In various places. For Amacron Thirty-seven I imagine the records are stored on Tallas Four. That's in the Orion sector. But you don't want to go there."

"Why not?" Adam asked.

Fur wrinkled his nose. "They have lousy food."

Adam and Watch looked at each other.

"Is there another reason we can't go to Tallas Four besides the lousy food?" Adam asked.

"Lots of reasons," Fur said. "It is a heavily fortified moon. Get within half a light-year of it and the Kaster will blow you out of the sky." He paused. "Why would you want to go there?"

"Isn't it obvious?" Adam asked. "We want to erase the record of our friends' debts."

Fur snorted. "That isn't going to happen."

Adam spoke in a stern voice. "If it doesn't happen you're not going to get our Kaster transporter."

Once again Fur lost his smile. "I can't take you to Tallas Four. Even my wonderful ship—the *Fruitfly*—

doesn't have a force field capable of withstanding what they would hit us with."

"But what if you had a Kaster force field surrounding your ship?" Watch asked.

Fur was instantly interested. "You have such a device?"

"We have a portable force field generator," Adam said quickly. "We don't know if it can protect your ship."

"If it's the one I'm thinking of, it can protect a whole battleship." Fur stuck out his white hand. "Let me see it."

Watch hesitated. "How do we know you'll give it back once we hand it over?"

"Because if I cheated you here in front of all these people my reputation would be permanently ruined. Don't worry, Watch. I just want to check its serial number."

Watch took out the oval-shaped generator and gave it to Fur, who studied it intently. Apparently the serial number was not something you read on the side of the object. But finally Fur's face brightened.

"You must have wished for the top of the line!" he exclaimed.

"Naturally," Watch said.

Fur continued. "The size of the field can be adjusted to accommodate the *Fruitfly*. The field can even be altered so that it makes my ship temporarily invisible. But that does not mean that we can simply break into Tallas Four and erase all the Kaster records. To do that we would have to blow up their computers—and that would take heavy fire power."

Watch pulled out the laser pistol. "Would this help?"

Fur was not impressed. "You didn't ask for the top of the line there. That's a beryllium laser. They're dependable but nothing special."

"Why can't we just beam ourselves to Tallas Four using the Kaster transporter?" Adam asked.

"Tallas Four is shielded, as is Amacron Thirty-seven. You cannot transport through a shield. You need to take a ship, and then the ship has to either sneak by the shield with another Kaster vessel, or else break through it directly." Fur shook his head. "Either way the chances of success are not good. Why don't I give you something else for the transporter and the portal generator? I would like them both. How about I give you my own house? I own an asteroid in the Taurus quadrant. You would have a great view of the Milky Way there, and the homeowner association charges are reasonable."

"Sounds like a workable deal," Watch said.

"No!" Adam exclaimed. "We have to rescue our friends. You either help us save them or there's no deal."

Fur smiled thinly. "If I help you, I will probably end up as dead as you will be. That doesn't sound like a good deal to me."

"It's the only deal we have to offer," Adam said. "Take it or leave it."

"Are you sure I couldn't interest you in a couple of Sirian pleasure robots? You can have them designed to your own specifications."

"We are too young to have girlfriends," Watch said.

"But Sally and Cindy are still very important to us," Adam added. "Even if they aren't real girlfriends."

Fur considered. "You would have to give me both the Kaster transporter and the Kaster force field."

"Fine," Adam said. "As long as you take us back to Earth after we wreck the Kaster records and rescue the girls."

Fur frowned and puffed on his cigar. "Are you sure you want to go back home? The food's lousy there as well." He added, "Except for your Cokes. I can drink six of those a day."

"Do we have a deal?" Adam asked.

Fur hesitated. "We will probably all die. I wasn't kidding."

Adam stuck out his hand. "Do we have a deal?"

Fur glanced around and then finally offered his hand. "I have a feeling I'm going to regret this," he said.

7

THE WORK SHIFT ON AMACRON 37 WAS hard. First the slaves were treated to a breakfast of cold, gluey porridge, and then they were herded into a stark warehouse where the Kaster lamps were assembled. Sally and Cindy were handed welding guns and dark goggles and told to get to work. A supervising robot stood not far away, its electric prod ready to shock any who were too slow. Cindy held up her welding gun.

"I don't know how to use this," she said.

"We better figure out quick or scrap metal over there is going to light us up like a Christmas tree," Sally said.

Fortunately Hironee appeared right then. The way she carried her welding gun, she looked like an expert.

"They have put you on the easy duty," she explained, pointing to the half-finished lamps in front of them. They were big by human standards, made of dark metal, very unattractive. "You just have to weld the lower four joints into place. A child can do it."

"That's good because we are only kids," Cindy said, feeling anxious.

Hironee turned and spoke to the closest robot. "I am going to show the humans how to perform their duties efficiently. Is that acceptable?"

"Efficient work is always acceptable," the robot replied.

"You just have to know how to talk to a robot," Hironee said, striking up her welding gun and pulling her dark goggles over her eyes. She bent down over the lamp in front of Sally. "You have to make sure the joint is firmly welded before you go on to the next one. Watch."

While Hironee worked, the girls stood behind her and spoke in low tones. Sally did most of the talking.

"How many robots are there in this particular camp?" she asked.

"Twenty," Hironee replied, the sparks of the welding gun spraying not far from her green face. "And then there's Teeh, who watches over them and us."

"The reptilian Kaster?" Sally asked.

"Yes. He's worse than a dozen robots put together."

"Do the robots have separate brains?" Sally asked. "Or are they all controlled from a central place?"

"Both," Hironee said. "They have individual positronic brains but they can be shut down from the computer in Teeh's office. But don't even dream of getting in there. It's heavily guarded."

"Is the force field that surrounds this camp controlled from there?" Sally asked.

"Yes."

"Did Charles bomb Teeh's office? Is that how he got through the force field?"

Hironee glanced behind them at the watching robot. "No. He bombed the field generator itself. If he had been able to bomb the office, the robots wouldn't have caught him so quickly and killed him. The computers would have crashed and the robots would have been disabled. But you must stop this line of thinking. I told you, no one can get close to Teeh's office."

Sally turned to Cindy. "We have to get in there. We have to disable the computer. It's the only way."

"But Hironee says that's impossible," Cindy protested.

"Do you want to stay here?" Sally demanded.

"No," Cindy said. "But I don't want to die either. But

even if we are able to flee into the desert, what are we going to do out there?"

"Adam and Watch will come for us," Sally said simply.

Cindy shook her head. "You're dreaming. They're on another part of the planet. Their situation is as lousy as ours."

"Hironee," Sally said. "If friends of ours were being sent here at the same time as us, would they have come here?"

"Were their wishes all placed on the same order?"

"Yes," Sally said. "The Collector specified that."

"Then they probably would have come here. But . . ." Hironee hesitated.

"What?" Cindy asked.

"If they resisted transportation they might have been killed back on Earth."

Cindy's lower lip quivered. "Oh no. That's probably what happened."

"Nonsense," Sally said impatiently. "A single Collector couldn't take out Adam and Watch. I'm sure Watch was able to shoot him with his laser. Then they probably took the transporter device. I bet they're on their way here now."

Hironee stopped welding and glanced up. "I told

you, this place is shielded. They couldn't transport here. They'd have to come in on a ship, a powerful ship."

"But if we escape this camp," Sally said, "they would be able to pick us up in the desert."

"*If* you can escape here," Hironee said. "*If* they are coming to your rescue. But those are two big ifs. You can't risk your life on them."

"I would rather die than be a slave the rest of my life," Sally said proudly.

"I would rather be home watching TV," Cindy said.

Hironee cautioned them to be silent. "Teeh is coming," she said.

The Kaster boss was as ugly as his reputation. He looked like a crocodile that had decided to stand upright. His thick tail flapped all over as he strode into the warehouse. He had a long snout and large teeth dripping saliva. He wore silver-colored armor over his chest. But the worst thing about him was that he sported his sunglasses at the end of his snout. For some reason they disturbed the girls more than anything else, possibly because they were so cheap and tacky. He waddled over to them.

"Are you the new slaves?" he asked in a slobbery voice.

"Yes, sir," Cindy said, standing stiffly, no doubt

worried about having her skin peeled off and eaten in front of her.

"We are Sally and Cindy," Sally said. "I am Sally."

"I am Cindy," Cindy said.

"How come you're not working?" he demanded.

"I was just showing them how to use the welding gun, sir," Hironee said.

Teeh was annoyed. "Did I ask you? Was I talking to you?"

"No, sir," Hironee said, lowering her head.

"We just got here," Sally said.

"I know that," Teeh said. "What do you think? I'm blind? I know everybody here." He leaned closer and studied Sally. "Where are the other two?"

"Which other two?" Cindy asked.

"Your friends," Teeh said. "Adam Freeman and Watch. They made wishes as well. I sent the Collector to fetch all four of you. Where are they?"

Cindy shrugged. "We don't know."

"I know," Sally said suddenly.

"Where?" Teeh asked, losing his patience.

Sally looked around as if they were being spied on. "I can't tell you here. We better talk in your office." She added, "It's a long story and the information could put you and your position in danger."

Teeh frowned, as best a standing crocodile could. "How can I be in danger?"

Sally leaned closer and spoke in his ear. "Only I can tell you. I am here to help you."

"Why should you, a human, help me?"

"Because I want to get ahead here," Sally said. "I don't mind stabbing my own people in the back."

Teeh stepped back and looked around as well. She had sized him up correctly; he was very paranoid and understood greed and ambition.

"Come with me to my office," he ordered and turned away.

Hironee looked at Sally with worried eyes as she was led away. Be careful, Sally."

"I know what I'm doing," Sally whispered in reply. But she looked scared.

8

THEY WERE IN DEEP SPACE, A FEW HOURS off Globar 92, with so many stars that Adam felt as if he had fallen into an alien's dream. The *Fruitfly* was not a large ship—the control room was no bigger than Adam's bedroom. The ceiling of the control room was clear as was the large viewing screen that Fur sat before. When Fur dimmed the lights it was easy to believe they were floating free without walls to protect them from endless space. Adam found the sensation exhilarating, as he did Fur's explanation of how they would get to Tallas 4.

"We have to move there through a series of hyper-jumps," Fur said as Watch and Adam listened closely. "Hyperspace is a region where the three dimensions of normal space can be folded into virtually no space. It makes interstellar travel possible. Without hyperjumps it would take centuries to journey between stars."

"Why do we have to make a series of jumps?" Watch asked. "Why not just one huge leap?"

"That is theoretically possible," Fur said, "but in practice it is dangerous. Gravity affects each hyperjump. That's why we had to plow away from Globar Ninety-two for as long as we have before attempting our first jump. We needed to get away from the sun and the asteroids. If we had tried to make a jump as soon as we left the asteroid, there would be no predicting where we would end up."

"Could we have materialized inside a star?" Adam asked.

Fur smiled. "It's possible but unlikely. Most of space is extremely empty. Probably we would have just ended up lost."

"So each time you make a jump," Watch said, "you recalculate what your next jump will be based on the gravitational influences in the immediate area?"

"Exactly," Fur said, reaching for his controls. "Now get ready, we are about to make the first jump. You might feel momentarily disoriented."

"I feel that way most of the time," Watch muttered.

CHRISTOPHER PIKE

Fur pushed a button and the stars outside suddenly rushed toward them at a dizzying speed. Then magically they vanished, and there was a moment of utter blackness, so deep Adam wasn't even sure if he was still alive. Just as quickly, the stars returned, but now they were not nearly so bright. Fur explained that they were now closer to the edge of the galaxy, where the stars were not so dense.

"Tallas Four is not far from here," Fur said. "The Kasters like to hide in places far from everyone else. We still have to make another two jumps to reach the moon."

"Are they ugly creatures?" Adam asked seriously.

"Not as ugly as human beings, if that's what you mean." Fur laughed. "Ugly is a relative term. Why, when you first met me I bet you thought I was ugly."

"No offense, but I still do," Watch said.

Fur stopped laughing. "I'll have you know I have had many dates with women from your planet and most of them were happy to get to know me."

"Where did you meet these women?" Adam asked.

"At Halloween parties."

"It figures," Watch muttered.

"And you just invited them over to see your spaceship?" Adam asked.

"Sure," Fur said. "I use that line. Works like a wonder."

"Why do you call your ship the *Fruitfly?*" Watch asked. "On Earth that would be considered a demeaning title."

Fur was offended. "On my home world fruit flies are considered quite a delicacy."

Adam was grossed out. "You mean you eat flies. Yuck!"

"They don't taste bad when you chase them down with a Coke," Fur said, his skillful hands working the controls. "Prepare for another jump. I am almost ready."

Over the next thirty minutes they made two more quick hyperjumps. Finally the large red gaseous planet around which Tallas 4 orbited came into view. Yet they knew it was large only because Fur said it was. They were still so far from it that it looked smaller than the moon as seen from Earth.

"But Tallas itself is ten times larger than your Jupiter," Fur explained as he turned the ship toward the planet and switched on the gravity drive that powered it through normal space.

"How long will it take to get there?" Adam asked.

"Four hours," Fur said.

"We can't jump the remainder of the distance?" Watch asked.

"No, for two reasons," Fur said. "It is too short a distance and in either case the force field surrounding Tallas would cause us to explode when we attempted to exit hyperspace."

"Have you installed the Kaster force field we loaned you?" Watch asked.

"Yes, but I don't want to use it to get through the planet's force field," Fur said. "I don't know if it's strong enough, and the Kasters watch the perimeter of this system closely. What I prefer to do is attach my ship to a small asteroid that flies near the Tallas defense field. If we use the *Fruitfly's* engines carefully, we should be able to alter the orbit of the asteroid slightly and fly close to Tallas without setting off any alarms. This system is thick with asteroids and we'll just be another big rock flying by."

"That's pretty clever," Watch said, impressed.

Fur smiled. "Do you still think I'm ugly, Watch?"

"You'd look good with a deep tan, a wig, and a pair of colored contacts," Watch said.

"But we'll have to break free of the asteroid to get to the moon?" Adam asked.

"Yes," Fur said. "Only then will we be able to turn on the force field and make ourselves invisible. The force field draws a lot of energy, so we can't keep it on too long."

"How are we going to blow up their computers?" Watch asked.

"We're not going to blow them up," Fur said.

"But we have to erase those debt records," Adam protested.

"There is no way we can use heavy firepower around this moon and not be destroyed," Fur said. "We would be spotted in a moment. My plan is to sneak onto the surface of the moon, find a terminal, and hopefully erase your friends' names from the computers. Kaster systems are always interlinked. Any terminal should give us access to all their records."

"And I suppose we can wear lizard makeup so that no one notices us?" Watch said sarcastically.

Fur was offended. "I have thought of that. Not everyone who works on Tallas Four is a Kaster. They have off-world help. That's what we will be."

"It sounds like a good plan to me," Adam said, trying to be supportive.

Fur took a while to find a suitable asteroid, one that was heading the right away and one that was bumpy enough to hide their small ship. They actually set down on the back side of the asteroid, and for a long time they couldn't see the red planet, Tallas, or the other four moons. But during that time Fur carefully applied the power of the ship's engines to the rear of the asteroid.

"This far out we only have to change its course slightly to cause it to fly inside the perimeter of the force field," he explained.

"Could the force field destroy the asteroid?" Watch asked.

"The asteroid should be able to absorb the energy and save us the shock. As soon as we're through we'll race toward Tallas Four."

Many hours later, as the asteroid finally began to contact the Kaster force field, the ship began to shake violently. It felt as if the ground where they had anchored were ready to explode. A wave of shimmering blue energy glittered in the space all around them. Adam hung on to his seat for dear life.

"This is a rough ride!" he shouted over the noise.

Fur laughed heartily. "This is nothing!"

The roller-coaster ride stopped a minute later. They were through the main force field. Yet they were still far from the moon, although for the first time they were able to see it, a dull orange-colored globe that was cold and uninviting. Fur continued to work the controls.

"We are turning on our invisibility cloak now," he said.

The view outside changed only slightly. It was as if a thin sheet of filmy material had been placed over the viewing screen, dulling the sky but not blocking it out. Fur fired the *Fruitfly*'s gravity engines and slowly they lifted off the asteroid. The feeling of slow motion may have only been an illusion. Because quickly enough the dull orange moon began to grow in size. Everything was going according to plan when suddenly there was a massive explosion behind them. They didn't hear it—because they were in the vacuum of space, which did not transmit sound waves—but they sure saw it. The explosion was blinding.

"What was that?" Adam gasped.

Fur sounded worried. "The asteroid. They fired on it."

"But why shoot at a rock?" Watch asked.

"Probably because they sensed someone was using it for the very purpose we just used it for," Fur said. "To get through the force field. If we hadn't taken off when we did we would be dead now." He paused. "I told you this was a risky mission."

"Risk is our middle name," Adam said proudly.

"I don't have a middle name," Watch said. "I can't even remember my last name."

"They will be alert now," Fur said. "Our only hope is that they assume we perished in the explosion."

"How come they can't penetrate their own cloaking device?" Watch asked.

"They could if they knew where to look," Fur said. "But they are probably not expecting anyone to try to land on Tallas Four."

"Why not?" Adam asked "Because of the food?"

"Because no one would be that stupid," Fur said grimly.

The orange moon continued to grow outside the view screen. Soon it dominated the sky, and Fur's hands were glued to the controls. He passed over what looked like a highly advanced city but shook his head when Watch asked if the computers could be located there.

"We will never find the computers themselves," Fur said. "They could be anywhere. We just need one terminal to tap into."

"Then why don't you just land anywhere?" Watch asked.

Obviously the tension was getting to Fur.

"Why don't you just sit quietly and let me do the flying, okay?" he snapped.

"I was just trying to make conversation," Watch muttered.

Fur dropped down low a few minutes later. For a moment it seemed they would crash, he was going in so swiftly. But at the last second he pulled up, and Adam felt his stomach go down to the floor. The orange terrain was now a blur. There were canyons and there were tall buildings. Moving so fast it was hard to tell one from the other. But just as quickly Fur brought them to a halt in a place so dark they could literally see nothing.

"Where are we?" Adam gasped.

"In somebody's garage," Fur said. "I spotted it on my instruments. They left it open and hopefully they're not home right now."

"You mean, we just landed in somebody's house?" Watch asked.

"Why not?" Fur asked. "All the houses here will have terminals." He stood up from his chair. "Let's hurry, we won't have long before we're spotted."

Of course the home Fur had chosen was not empty. Two irritated crocodile creatures rushed at them the moment they stepped inside the Kaster home. Watch had to draw his laser pistol and stun them. Yet the Kaster creatures continued to flap their tails even in their unconscious state. Fur stepped over them nonchalantly.

"You can say what you want about them," Fur said, "but they are neat housekeepers."

The home was gorgeous, in fact, the towering rooms filled with frequent waterfalls, dark pools. It seemed the

Kasters liked to spend a lot of time in water, like croco-
diles back on Earth.

Fur found a computer terminal and sat down. He
turned the machine on and slipped what looked like a
thumb drive in a side panel. The computer screen and
the keyboard were much larger and more complex than
human components. Fur explained as he worked.

"The software I have inserted into their system was
written by a form of bacteria on Demavon One Hundred Twenty-three. Those bacteria are really smart—
everyone goes to them for their computer games. This
program will trace back to the Kasters' main computers. The program is great at getting into supposedly
impenetrable files."

"We could use that kind of bacteria on Earth," Watch
said. "Our computer games are getting boring."

"They tried to visit your world once," Fur said. "But
they just ended up giving a New York cab driver a chest
cold. He went to the doctor and got a shot of penicillin
and that wiped out the whole Demavon One Hundred
Twenty-three expedition." Fur stopped and laughed. "I
bet the cab driver didn't realize what kind of money he
gave up with that one shot. The bugs could have taught
him how to program his yellow cab to make hyper-
jumps."

"It is upon such small and insignificant incidents that the destinies of worlds turn," Watch observed.

Fur let out a sound of joy. "I'm in their records! Quick, how do you spell Sally and Cindy's full names?"

"Sally is officially Sara Wilcox," Adam said. "That's Sara without an *h*. Cindy is Cynthia Makey. Do you need help with any of those spellings?"

"No," Fur said, still excited. "I'm calling up their records now. And in a few seconds I should be able to erase them from the system by putting in another Demavon One Hundred Twenty-three program designed for just such a purpose. Then we can be out of here and on our way to Amacron Thirty-seven with a clean slate for your friends."

"Both Adam and I have a little debt as well," Watch said.

Fur nodded. "I suspected as much. How do you spell your last name, Watch?"

"I don't think even the Kasters know that," Adam muttered.

Five minutes later Fur was not so confident. He had put in another program and gotten trapped in a complex web of information. It was only after minutes of fighting with the computer that realization struck and Fur leapt to his feet.

"They must be onto us!" he exclaimed. "They are just feeding me this garbage to make me think I'm getting closer to getting rid of the records. But it's hopeless; we have to get out of here." He turned in the direction they had entered. Adam grabbed his arm, stopping him.

"But we have come so far," Adam pleaded. "We can't quit now."

Fur brushed off his hand. "Don't you see, Adam, they are tracking us this very moment, back to this terminal. If we don't get off this moon in the next few seconds we will all end up on a slave planet." Fur suddenly stopped. There was a banging outside. "What was that?"

"Sounds like a gang of Kaster police pounding on the front door," Watch said.

Fur stuck out his hand. "Give me your laser pistol."

"What will you trade me in return?" Watch asked.

"Our lives," Adam said. "Just give it to him. What are you going to do, Fur?"

Fur grabbed the weapon from Watch and began to fiddle with the controls. "This can be set to overload. When it does, it makes a respectable blast." He stalked toward the door to the bedroom. "When you hear the explosion, run for the ship. Don't look left or right, just keep running." Fur opened the door. "It's time to show the Kaster cops what your human trick-or-treat means."

Adam and Watch looked at each other.

"How do we get in situations like this?" Adam asked.

"We keep poor company," Watch replied.

"Sally?"

"Sally is dangerous," Watch said. "She's worse than the Kasters."

"But she does make our lives more exciting."

"That's true," Watch agreed.

There was a massive explosion. It was so powerful, so deafening, that Adam and Watch were sure Fur had perished trying to stop the Kasters. But they remembered his last instruction, to run for his ship no matter what, and that's what they did. But they had to run through smoke and fire to get there. The two Kaster homeowners were just reviving but were still unable to chase them. They were more than a little relieved to find Fur already at the controls of *Fruitfly* when they got safely aboard.

"What happened?" Adam gasped.

Fur grinned. "I answered the door and politely asked them what they wanted. They didn't even reply. They immediately opened fire." He added, "I didn't tell you that I had removed the force field generator and carried it into the house in my pocket. Their laser beams bounced back on them and caused their whole load of weapons to explode."

CHRISTOPHER PIKE

"You carried the force field on your own body so that you would be safe," Watch said.

"Hey," Fur said. "I'm the only one here who can fly this ship. That makes me the most valuable person. Anyway, I have hooked the generator back up to the ship." Fur nodded at the mess out the forward viewing screen. "We're going to need it like we never needed it before. Especially in the next two minutes."

"If we fly into orbit they'll just blow us out of the sky," Adam said as Fur started the ship's engines. Fur's hands flew over the controls.

"We're not going to stay around long enough for them to take aim," Fur said.

"You're going to hyperjump as soon as we're in space," Watch said, excited at the prospect.

"Exactly," Fur said. "Hold on."

"But you said such a jump is uncontrollable!" Adam shouted as he was pressed back into his seat by the force of the acceleration. They roared out of what was left of the Kaster garage. The haunting orange sky loomed above them. But very quickly it began to darken, as they plowed beyond the atmosphere and into space.

"Better an uncontrollable jump than certain death!" Fur yelled back. He glanced above as they broke completely free of the atmosphere. Mixed in with the stars were three Kaster warships rushing toward them. "Prepare to jump!"

"But we still need to get to Amacron Thirty-seven!" Adam yelled. "We have to rescue the girls!"

"We rescue ourselves first!" Fur yelled.

And with that they jumped into hyperspace.

With no idea where they would end up.

9

SALLY STOOD IN TEEH'S OFFICE AND WON-
dered what she was going to tell the Kaster boss. So
intent had she been on just getting to the heart of
the compound's power that she hadn't planned how
she was going to get out of the office. Teeh, still
slobbering and still wearing his cheap sunglasses, sat
down across from her. There was no other chair and
he didn't offer to get her one. The crocodile boss put
his scaly feet up on his dirty desk and looked at her
as if she had better have a good reason for requesting
a private audience.

"Well?" he said. "Where are your friends?"

Sally swallowed. "They're not here."

"I know they're not here. Do I look stupid or what? Where are they?"

"They're on their way here," she said.

"What are you talking about?"

"Has the Collector you sent to fetch us returned?"

"I ask the questions here!" Teeh paused. "No. It hasn't."

"Adam and Watch destroyed it."

Teeh sat up straight. "How do you know this?"

Sally felt herself getting in the mood to tell some really great lies.

It was a special feeling of power.

"I know them. They're very powerful. At this moment they have allied themselves with other powerful beings and are on their way here to rescue Cindy and me."

Teeh snorted. "You're dreaming. No one tries to rescue anyone from Amacron Thirty-seven. It's a dust bowl—hardly anyone can even find this place."

"Then where is your Collector?" Sally asked.

Teeh scratched his scaly head. "I don't know. I suppose it is possible your friends got the upper hand with him. What is it they ordered anyway?"

"Watch ordered a laser pistol and a personal force field generator." Sally added, "He also got himself a telescope."

Teeh frowned. "We have to stop offering those personal force field generators. We lose more Collectors that way." He paused and studied her. "Why are you telling me all this?"

"I told you, I want to get ahead. And I don't mind betraying my friends to do it. I tell you seriously, they are on their way here this very minute. If you don't take care, you'll be removed as boss of this planet."

"Who are the powerful beings they have made friends with?"

Sally darkened her expression. "The *Treeboards*."

"I haven't heard of them. What sector are they from?"

"They don't even come from this galaxy. They're from a black hole at the edge of the universe. They're an ancient race. They were highly evolved when your race and mine were bacteria swimming in primeval mud. They have powers we can't even dream of."

"Then what would they want with your friends?"

Sally spoke in a whisper. "They have allied themselves with Adam and Watch because they have a common goal. You see, the Treeboards have an ancient and undying hatred for ugly lizards like—for reptilian superraces like yours. Adam and Watch have stolen your Collector's transporter. They have an easy way to get here now, and the evil Treeboards want to come along for the ride, to destroy you. To destroy all Kasters, wherever they may be." Sally paused for effect. "The shield you have erected around Amacron Thirty-seven will not stop them. It won't even come close."

Teeh appeared unsure of himself. "This story sounds outlandish. Can you prove that these Treeboards even exist?"

"Yes. I spent time with them on a lost moon circling a dead quasar ten billion light-years from here. They taught me many of their secrets, and I can show you some of those secrets now. I can teach you how to strengthen the force field that surrounds this planet so that even the Treeboards—even Watch or Adam— cannot get through with their fleet of super-tachyon spaceships."

Teeh raised an eyebrow. "What are those?"

"Highly developed vessels that you'll never see in a Collector's Christmas catalog. Listen to me, Teeh, please, I am the only one who can save you. If you'll just give me a few minutes with your computer, I can prove it to you."

Teeh considered. "What do you want in return for this help?"

"You must erase my Wishing Stone debt."

"What about the debt of your friend, Cindy?"

Sally waved her hand. "She is of no concern to me. She can rot here for the rest of eternity, for all I care."

Teeh grinned. She had hit the right nerve. He was now convinced.

"Spoken like a true Kaster," he said. "Are you sure you don't have reptilian blood in your veins, Sally?"

"My grandmother always used to say my grandfather was a snake. I never met him, but I heard the stories. He was your kind of man, Teeh. And I am your girl. Where's your computer?"

Teeh stood and moved toward an elaborate control panel. "You understand that while you work on my computer I must supervise you?"

Sally followed him to the computer. It looked like a bunch of lights and buttons to her. She wished Watch was with her now.

"Naturally," she said. "It is my hope I can teach you a few things." She added, "I mean that with all due respect, of course."

"Of course," Teeh said, in a good mood, for him. "You are familiar with my operating system? The famous Kaster double matrix algorithm TEC dot software?"

Sally waved her hand as she sat down in front of the massive computer. "I learned about that when I was in first grade. It is an extremely primitive system when compared to what the Treeboards use." Sally touched the keyboard and then paused. "I need an electric stick."

"What?"

"One of those sticks your primitive robots carry. I need one."

"What for?"

"I am going to link it into your computer system so that this whole planet will be transformed into one cosmic-size electric stick capable of repelling the super-tachyon fleet that races toward this planet at this very instant." Sally had to pause to catch her breath. "Do you have one in your desk?"

Teeh turned back to his desk. "I believe so. But frankly this kind of technology confuses me. I have never seen anything like it."

"Neither have I," Sally whispered.

"What?"

"Nothing. Everything will become clear quickly. The power of your protective shield will change beyond your wildest dreams. With this technology, you will be the single most powerful Kaster in this section of the galaxy."

Teeh found an electric stick in one of his drawers. "I have not had the advantage of your obviously extensive education. How long will it take me to comprehend the Treeboard technology?"

"A sly lizard like—I mean, a brilliant Kaster—like you will know more than I do before we leave this room." She stuck out her hand and took the electric stick. "Now I just need to know one other thing."

Teeh stood nearby. "What?"

"Where does this computer plug in?"

"What do you mean?"

"Its power source. Where does it draw its power from?"

Teeh nodded to a black box at the side of the control panel. "From there. Do you need more power? I can have extra cables run in."

"Maybe. Open the power box. Let me study it."

Teeh did so. It looked much like a fuse box back home.

Sally turned on the electric stick and got up. "Stand aside, Teeh."

He did as she requested but a flicker of doubt crossed his face.

"What are you doing?" he asked.

"Changing the polarity of the situation." Sally rammed the tip of the electric stick into the black box. The thing literally exploded in sparks. She knew immediately the damage was enough to knock out the force field and all the robots. She turned the stick on Teeh and smiled wickedly up at his blustering expression. "I am changing everything," she said.

He was enraged. "You will pay for this!"

"Wrong! We're through paying!"

And with that Sally stuck the electric stick up his fat snout.

Teeh turned a deeper green than normal and fainted.

Sally stepped on his cheap sunglasses as she fled the room.

10

THEY CAME OUT OF HYPERSPACE IN THE center of the galaxy. There were so many stars that it was almost impossible to find any black space. Fur quickly handed them each a pair of black sunglasses. Watch stared out the viewing screen, enthralled.

"I'll never see anything like *this* in my telescope," he said.

"If we don't get out of here quick we won't be seeing period," Fur said.

"Why not?" Adam asked.

"There are tremendous levels of radiation at the galactic core," Fur explained. "Our force field is keeping them at bay for the moment but that won't last.

The first thing this level of radiation burns is the optic nerves."

"Can we make a hyperjump so close to all these stars?" Watch asked.

Fur was grim. "We have no choice. But it could tear us apart."

"We will go out in a blaze of glory," Watch said, still staring at the stars.

"What glory?" Adam asked. "We failed in our quest. We weren't able to destroy the records on Tallas Four. Our debts will last forever. We will never be free of them."

"Isn't there a saying on your world?" Fur asked as he worked the controls. "'It ain't over till it's over'? That's my motto. Hold on, we're going to make another jump, and I can guarantee this one will be rough."

They leapt into hyperspace, and the jump was different from the others. Not really rough, but it seemed as if the period of blackness lasted forever. During that time Adam wondered if they wouldn't be trapped for eternity outside of normal space and time. But finally the stars reappeared and Fur quickly checked his navigation computer.

"I know where we are!" he exclaimed.

"Where?" Adam asked.

"In the Beta quadrant—not far from Amacron Thirty-seven." He paused. "Are you sure you still want to go there? We'll never get through their force fields. Slave planets are strictly off-limits."

"We have to try," Adam said.

"But we can always try later," Watch said.

"Watch!" Adam complained. "I'm disappointed in you."

"I would rather live with your disappointment than die in a Kaster force field," Watch replied. But then he paused and gave it some thought. "But I suppose we might succeed in the end. We usually do." He nodded to Fur. "Plot a hyperjump for Amacron Thirty-seven."

"And may the Force be with us," Adam said.

"*Star Wars,*" Fur quipped. "Great movie."

A few minutes later they were again flying through hyperspace.

When Sally ran from Teeh's office, she immediately saw that her plan had worked. The robot guards were all immobilized. Yet her plan had its limits, as Cindy had pointed out. There was nowhere to go except into the desert.

Cindy and Hironee came out of the work warehouse as Sally ran over. The other slaves were still inside, casting hesitant looks in their direction. They had nothing else to do now that the power was off all over the compound.

"What's happened?" Hironee asked.

"I disabled the computer," Sally said. "That means the force field is down for the time being. We have to get out of here before it comes back online."

"But what happened to Teeh?" Cindy asked.

"He's taking a nap," Sally said.

"A nap?" Hironee asked, puzzled.

"With an electric toothpick up his nose. Look, we can talk about this once we're deep in the desert and clear of the force field."

Cindy nodded. "I'll get us water bottles and pack some supplies." She dashed off to collect the stuff. For the moment Sally was left alone with Hironee and a robot that stood perfectly still nearby, caught in mid-stride by the drop in power. Sally was surprised that Hironee wasn't excited and asked her what the problem was. The green girl answered with her head down.

"We can't go into the desert," she said softly. "Charles went into the desert and he died."

Sally put a hand on her shoulder. "Charles didn't knock out the robots like we have. They were the ones who hunted him down and killed him. Also, Charles was alone. In the desert we can help each other." Sally paused. "Something else is bothering you."

Hironee nodded weakly. "I hate this place. I've told you how much I hate it. But I've been here half my life. It's home to me now. I know that sounds silly but I'm afraid to leave it." She stopped and Sally saw the tears in her eyes. "You and Cindy had better leave without me."

"Nonsense. We'll never do that." Sally gave her a hug and then gestured to the barren landscape. "This is no home for a person like you. Try to remember what Zanath was like—the blue water, the green islands, the warm yellow sun in the clear sky. That's your home, Hironee, and if you come with us you might see it again soon. I'm not promising you will. Maybe you will die in the desert like Charles—that's a definite possibility. But you have to know deep inside that it's better to die free than to live as a slave."

Hironee smiled. "You never told me, Sally, that you were a motivational speaker."

Sally laughed. "My talents are endless." She turned toward the building where Cindy had disappeared. "Let's take what supplies we can carry and get out of here before Lizard Breath wakes up."

They came out of hyperspace much closer to Amacron 37 than they had been to the other worlds when they had finished making their jumps. Fur explained that he had intentionally cut it close so that the Kasters would have less time to spot them.

"But we can circle around the planet until they shoot us down if we're hoping to get into their slave compounds," he said gloomily as they raced toward the desert planet, a purple sun hanging in the sky off to their right.

"Are the force fields just around the slave compounds?" Watch asked.

"Usually," Fur said. "There's no point in protecting all of a planet like this. It's mostly dust and sand. The Kasters usually concentrate their energy where it's needed most. But that allows them to erect an even stronger force field. Don't fool yourself, this place is more protected than Tallas Four was."

"Where we were far from a huge success," Watch observed.

"Is there no way to get through the force fields?" Adam asked, frustrated.

"We can try," Fur said. "We can turn Watch's generator up to full power and try to smash through. But there is an excellent chance we'll explode."

"Better not risk it," Watch said, having second thoughts.

"We have to give it a try," Adam said.

Fur stared at him. "These two girls must be pretty special."

"One of them is," Watch said. "The other is just unusual."

"They are our friends," Adam said. "That's what matters."

Fur was wistful. "I wish I had friends as loyal as you two." He added, "Or at least as loyal as you, Adam." Something on the control panel caught his eye. He pushed a couple of buttons, seemingly rechecking his readings. "This is odd."

"What is it?" Adam asked.

"The southernmost compound on Amacron Thirty-seven—its force field is shut down. Not only that, there are three life forms heading away from the compound, heading into the deep desert."

"It must be the girls!" Adam exclaimed.

"I thought there were only two of them," Fur said.

"They make friends fast," Watch said. "At least Cindy does."

Something else on the control panel caught Fur's eye. But rather than try to ascertain what it was with his instruments, he leaned back and stared up at the window on the ceiling of the control room. Adam and

Watch did the same just in time to see a fleet of warships materialize in normal space. Clearly the ships had just completed a jump through hyperspace. They were gray in color, long and sleek, with red fins and smoldering weapons ports.

"The Kasters," Fur said softly, stunned. "They must have followed us here from Tallas Four."

"They could trace us through hyperspace?" Watch asked.

Fur shook his head. "No. But they didn't have to. They figured we were coming here because we were trying to erase records related to Amacron Thirty-seven."

"Do we have to surrender?" Adam asked.

Fur was grim. "The Kasters do not take prisoners in a situation like this."

"Then we must try to jump into hyperspace again," Watch said.

"No," Adam said. "We have to get the girls first."

"If we land, we will be completely helpless," Fur said. "They will destroy us at their leisure. I agree with Watch. We must try to escape." Fur started to push the button that would launch them into hyperspace. But Adam stopped him by putting a hand on his arm.

"The girls have knocked out the Amacron Thirty-seven force field when you said that was impossible,"

Adam said. "They are out in the desert, fighting for their lives, for freedom. How can we just abandon them when they have fought so hard and we are so close to them?"

Watch spoke up. "Adam has a point. Even I would feel guilty leaving them at this point."

Fur studied his instruments. "They are not alone in the desert. A force of robots is now following them." He looked at them. "If we land we will have enemies on all sides."

Adam didn't hesitate. "Land. We either save them or we all die together."

Watch patted Fur on the back and tried to reassure the trader. "We're all from Spooksville. We have an excellent track record in hopeless situations."

Fur sighed. "I don't."

11

HIRONEE SAW THE *FRUITFLY* FIRST. THEY
were trudging around a massive sand dune when the
ship appeared in the sky above them, burning with the
flames of reentry, heading straight for them like a meteor
shot from a cannon.

"Look!" Hironee shouted.

Sally and Cindy almost fell over when they saw the
ship.

"Is it a Kaster vessel?" Sally asked, fully expecting the
answer to be yes.

Hironee squinted. "No, I don't think so. It looks
more like a trader ship."

Sally looked at Cindy. "It could be Adam and Watch."

Cindy nodded anxiously. "Hope so."

But then abruptly all hope faded because the fleet of Kaster warships—chasing the trader vessel—became visible at the same time Teeh and his robots rounded the sand dune behind the girls. The Kaster warships had torpedo tubes on both sides that glowed a wicked red. Teeh had a small fleet of powerful ground vehicles that resembled open-air tanks. Both Kaster groups seemed to be ready to take aim, yet perhaps Teeh, seeing the ships overhead, warned his robots off. The slimy boss probably didn't want to get blasted with the humans. Overhead the ships suddenly veered off. Yet they didn't fly away, but rather, began to swoop in at a low altitude.

In the meantime the trader ship landed.

Adam and Watch and a ghost character with a bald head and a cigar jumped out. The girls ran to the boys and embraced them.

"Are we glad to see you!" Cindy exclaimed, giving Adam a big hug.

"We're happy to see you, too!" Adam said, hugging her back.

"I was the one who disabled the Kaster force field," Sally said quickly.

"I was the one who blew up part of the Kaster house," Fur said, watching both the approaching land army and the hovering warships. "But it looks like we both managed to anger the wrong people."

"And who may I ask are you?" Sally asked suspiciously.

Fur bowed. "I am Fur and I am here to rescue you." He glanced at Watch. "This must be the unusual one."

"I knew you would spot her immediately," Watch said.

"I will have you know that it was I who said you were on your way here to rescue us," Sally said. "While Cindy here was ready to bury you, as usual, I might add."

Fur gestured to the approaching armored car, which carried several robots and the grand master of slobberers himself—the Kaster boss, Teeh. His snout looked swollen and sore. He held a black laser rifle in his two stubby arms.

"I think we might all be buried in a few minutes," Fur said.

Teeh parked a few feet away and his group of robots immediately jumped from the armored vehicle and surrounded the other six. Mean-looking lasers were pointed at their heads. Teeh also approached. Although he carried a weapon, his free hand kept moving to his bruised snout. He went straight to Sally and glared at her.

"I am going to peel you alive!" he swore. "I will swallow your flesh before your very eyes! You will die with your own screams in your ears!"

Sally spoke sweetly. "Did the Treeboards hurt your nose, Mr. Teeh?"

Teeh growled. "There are no Treeboards!"

"Of course there are," Watch said. "All boards come from trees."

"I know that!" Teeh said. "Do I look stupid or something? I—"

"You do look stupid," Cindy interrupted, surprising them all. She just shrugged when they stared at her. "He looks like a stupid crocodile from a dirty swamp. What can I say?"

Teeh was not amused. "You will pay for that!"

Sally snorted. "I told you, we're through paying. If you're going to kill us, kill us now and get it over with. We're not afraid to die."

"I would like to mention that Sally does not speak for all of us," Watch said.

"I would like to second that," Fur said.

Just then one of the Kaster warships settled to the ground behind the *Fruitfly*. The vessel was massive, powerful; it cast a steaming shadow over the entire area. An official-looking Kaster captain with a host of lizard guards approached, making a mess of the sand dune with their swishing tails. The captain clearly outranked Teeh, who quickly bowed to the commander of the warship.

"Captain Thorath," Teeh said. "A pleasure. What brings you to Amacron Thirty-seven?"

Captain Thorath pointed a scaly finger at Fur. "This trader invaded Tallas Four and tried to wipe out several debt records from our computer files. I am here to arrest him and bring him back to Tallas Four for immediate trial and execution."

"At least you get a trial," Watch said to Fur.

"I may have trouble finding an impartial jury, though," Fur said.

"What about these other two humans?" Teeh asked Captain Thorath, pointing to Adam and Watch. Captain Thorath did not answer immediately. He seemed to be caught off guard by the question. He studied Adam and Watch, seemingly trying to figure out a problem that was bothering him.

"Which one of you is Adam?" he asked finally.

"I am," Adam said.

"Tell him what a slob he is," Sally said in his ear. "Don't let him intimidate you."

"Shh," Adam cautioned.

Captain Thorath stepped closer to Adam. The

commander appeared to be still puzzled over what to do next, what to say. "You made an unusual wish with one of our stones," he said finally.

"I wished for galactic peace," Adam said.

"You did?" Fur said with interest.

"Yes," Adam said sadly. He gestured to the warships and the armed robots that continued to point at them with their weapons. "But it doesn't look like my wish will be granted anytime soon."

"But it must be granted," Fur said with excitement in his tone.

Captain Thorath quickly held up a scaly hand. "We need not go into that right now," he said.

Fur stepped forward. "But you know the rules, Commander. The whole galaxy knows them." Fur turned back to Adam. "Tell me, was your wish on the same order as the others?"

"This is nonsense," Teeh interrupted, speaking to the warship commander. "Let's kill them all now and eat their skins."

"His wish was on the same order," Sally said to Fur. "The Collector stated that fact."

Fur smiled and turned to Captain Thorath. "Then you cannot collect on any of their wishes. Not until every wish on the order has been granted. Those are your own rules written by your own senate."

"We don't grant the wishes until the debts have been paid off," Teeh said bitterly.

Fur shook his head. "Your commander knows better. You grant the wishes, then collect the debts, then give the stuff back when the debts have been paid off." He added with bitterness, "Of course you never really have to give anything back. All your slaves die before they have a chance to collect."

"As well they should," Teeh said. "Do we look like we're stupid? We—"

"Shut up, Teeh," Captain Thorath told the slave boss. He spoke to the gang. "It is true what your trader friend says. We cannot legally collect on your debts until all the wishes on the same order have been granted. But, Adam, because your wish is so unusual, we doubt if we will ever be able to grant it." He paused. "For that reason we would prefer you make another wish. Something simple, easy to make in a factory."

"But if I do that then we will all end up as slaves," Adam said.

Captain Thorath sighed. "I was afraid you'd say that." He spread his hands. "Then what should we do? I am open to suggestions."

Fur spoke to the gang. "Don't do anything. Let the

wish for galactic peace remain. Then the Kasters will be obligated to fulfill it before they can come after you again. And that wish will never be granted, especially by the Kasters. They are always at war with somebody."

"But we can't let these humans go!" Teeh broke in. "This one here electrocuted my snout!"

"Good for her," Captain Thorath muttered, thinking, his gaze far away. Finally he turned back to the gang. "Very well, a rule is a rule, and we shouldn't be breaking our own if we expect others to listen to them." He drew in a deep breath. "You are not obligated to pay your debts until all the wishes on your order have been fulfilled."

"Which in practice means you won't have to ever pay them," Fur said.

"Do we get to keep the things we wished for?" Sally asked.

Captain Thorath hesitated. "Yes."

Sally squealed with delight. "I knew what I was doing all along! I'm rich!"

But Captain Thorath pointed at Fur and Hironee. "But this trader is coming back to Tallas Four with me, to be tried and executed. And, Teeh, you can do what you wish with this disobedient slave."

"I will eat her flesh in front of her eyes!" Teeh exclaimed.

Hironee cowered. "No."

"Get over the flesh thing already," Sally muttered. She put her arm around Hironee's shoulders and spoke to the commander. "You can't hurt our friend. We won't let you."

Fur looked anxiously around. "Why isn't anyone hugging me?"

Teeh gloated at Sally. "We can do whatever we want with both of them."

Adam took another step forward. "Wait a second. Captain Thorath, between the four of us we wished for some pretty expensive items. We got money, force fields, a new telescope, new outfits. These things must have cost the Kasters a pretty penny."

Captain Thorath studied him. "What is your point, young man?"

"What if we give you back all these things?" Adam said. "And in exchange you let Hironee and Fur go?"

Sally took her arm off Hironee. "Don't give the money back," Sally whispered to Adam.

"I really like that telescope," Watch said.

"Your proposition is an interesting one," Captain Thorath said. "A dead trader is of little use to us, and I am sure Teeh here has plenty of slaves to eat." He paused. "I will accept your offer to return the goods, as long as you can all agree on the offer."

"I agree," Fur said.

"You don't count," Sally snapped at him. "I say we return everything except the money and Hironee gets to go free with us."

"But Fur is our friend," Adam protested.

"Well . . . we haven't known him all that long," Watch added.

Adam held up his hands. "Wait a second! How can we have galactic peace if we can't even have peace among ourselves? We're all friends here. We have to stick together like friends should. We either return everything and all go free or else remain here and labor away until the end of our lives." He paused for effect. "What's it going to be?"

Watch shrugged. "I already have a pretty good telescope at home."

"I say we give all the stuff back," Cindy said.

Sally hesitated. "I suppose I'll get rich anyway, either as a famous actress or a best-selling novelist."

Adam smiled and offered his hand to Captain Thorath. "It's a deal."

Captain Thorath shook Adam's hand and nodded. "You continue to think big, Adam. The galaxy needs more people like you."

Hironee turned to Sally. "I get to return to Zanath?"

Sally hugged her. "Yeah, and your ticket's costing me a couple of million. But don't let that bother you. I just mention it in passing."

Fur beamed and puffed on his cigar. "I can take you back to Zanath. Heck, I can take the rest of you back to Earth." He turned toward his spaceship, and the rest of them followed. "I've got to see this famous Spooksville. It sounds like a happening place."

Sally glanced one last time at desolate Amacron 37 and turned up her nose.

"Yeah," she said. "It sure beats this place."

TURN THE PAGE FOR A SNEAK PEEK AT
SPOOKSVILLE #10: THE WICKED CAT

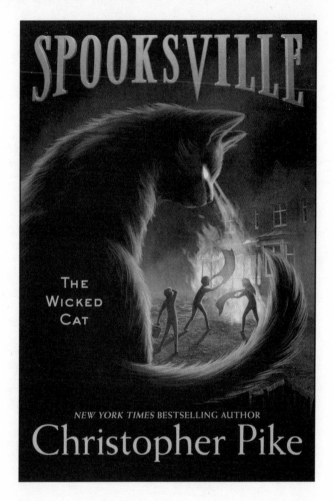

THE BLACK CAT WAS WAITING FOR THEM ON the path.

They weren't far outside of town when they bumped into it. Lately, because they'd been running into so much trouble in the woods and hills surrounding Spooksville, they had stayed closer to town. Actually, a lot of days they never even left the city. The whole summer they'd had adventure after adventure, and even though they'd enjoyed most of them—after they were over—they felt that each adventure was making them old before their time. Watch especially had gotten tired of risking his life, and said he had a new goal—to live long enough to get his driver's license.

"They'll never give you a driver's license," Sally Wilcox said as they walked on a path just east of the cemetery, which wasn't a bad spot if you liked glorious views of a witch's castle and tons of tombstones. Spooksville had a much higher death rate than birth rate. Sally brushed aside her dark bangs and continued, "You can't see well enough to pass the eye test."

"I've thought of that," Watch, who seemed to have been born without a last name, said. He always wore four watches—two on an arm, each set for a different time zone in the country. "But I plan to memorize the chart beforehand."

"That would be cheating," Cindy Makey, always one to be worried about what was right and proper, said. She had long blond hair and was very pretty.

"The means justify the end," Watch said.

"But you might still have trouble driving," Adam Freeman reminded him gently. Adam, who usually led the group, was short with dark hair. He worried about his height and doing the right thing. "If you can't see the road and all."

"Yeah, you might run over little kids like old Harry Hit and Run," Sally said.

"I won't be like him," Watch said.

"Why? What did he do?" Cindy asked.

"His name sort of explains it all, don't you think?" Sally replied, always trying to put Cindy down.

"He was an old guy who used to drive around in a boat-size black Cadillac and tried to run kids over," Watch said. "If you saw him coming, you had to get out of his way. He didn't care if you were on the sidewalk or not, he'd speed up and try to hit you."

"Did he ever kill anyone?" Adam asked, horrified.

"Dozens," Sally answered solemnly.

"I can't remember anyone specific," Watch corrected. "But he sure tried his best all the time. One day his nastiness got the best of him. He ran into a telephone pole and when it fell down on him, he was electrocuted."

"The kids in town didn't want him buried," Sally said. "We all signed a petition to hang him on the town Christmas tree that year. He glowed in the dark and actually looked better dead than alive."

Cindy shook her head. "I can't believe you hung a corpse on a Christmas tree."

"Wait till you see some of the Christmas presents people give each other in this town," Sally said wisely. "Then you'll see that a corpse is nothing."

"What happened to Harry's Cadillac?" Adam asked.

"It seems Harry had possessed it," Watch said. "It drove down to Hollywood and tried to get bit parts in horror films. I've seen it in a few movies that went straight to video. It got itself a new paint job and is now bright red."

"A car can't be possessed," Cindy said, annoyed.

"If kids with good grades can be possessed," Sally said, "a car can be."

It was just then that they noticed the cat sitting on the path in front of them.

What impressed Adam most about it was how shiny its black fur was. The cat looked groomed by a professional. Also, it had intense green eyes that glowed as bright as any Christmas light. As it stared at them, Adam felt as if he were being examined from the inside out. To be quite honest, he took an immediate dislike to the cat. But he didn't say that to the others because it sounded stupid to take a personal dislike to an animal. Especially when Sally seemed so taken with it.

"Wow," Sally said, stopping them. "Look at that cat. It looks like a princess or something the way it's sitting there."

"But it's a black cat," Cindy said. "Isn't it supposed to be unlucky to have a black cat cross your path?"

"That's just superstition," Adam answered her.

"But since every other superstition in the book seems

to be true in Spooksville we might want to watch it," Watch said.

"Nonsense," Sally replied. "It's a beautiful cat. Look at the way it's watching us. And it doesn't have a collar. Maybe it's a stray and doesn't belong to anyone."

"You know you don't have a good history with the things you find to take home," Watch said, referring to the Wishing Stone, which had almost got all of them stranded on a slave planet for the rest of their miserable lives.

"A cat can't be dangerous," Sally said. "Look, I think she likes me."

"You suffer from a strange belief that everyone likes you," Cindy muttered.

Sally took a step forward. "Here kitty, kitty, kitty. Come to Sally."

It seemed Sally was right. The cat immediately walked over and licked Sally's hands as she knelt to greet it. Watch leaned over and spoke to Adam.

"I think it must be a very tolerant cat," he said.

"I heard that," Sally muttered. "Any of you guys got any food on you?"

"Like I always carry a can of tuna in my back pocket," Cindy said.

Adam stepped to Sally's side. "It looks like it's well fed," he said, "so it must belong to someone."

"Then how come it doesn't have a collar on?" Sally asked.

"You don't wear a collar and you belong to someone," Watch said.

"I'm trying to help out a stray animal here," Sally said. "Why are you guys giving me such a hard time?"

"We're just jealous that the cat likes you and doesn't like us," Cindy said sarcastically.

The cat stared at her with its bright green eyes and Sally smiled.

"Animals can see the inner person," Sally said. "They don't judge people by exterior traits."

"This cat must be as blind as me," Watch said.

"If you take it home with you and feed it," Adam warned Sally, "you might have trouble getting rid of it."

Sally stood with the cat snuggled in her arms. Actually, it was sort of a big cat to carry. Adam couldn't help noticing how sharp its claws were. He was more of a dog person himself. He'd had to leave his dog in Kansas City when they moved from there to Spooksville. He still missed Lucky, who had been a sweet old mutt.

"Why should I want to get rid of it?" Sally asked.

"Your parents might not want it," Cindy said.

"But if I scream just right and throw a fit they'll warm to it," Sally said.

"I'm still worried it might belong to someone else," Adam said. "The owner could be hiking somewhere out here, not far from us. Why don't you put the cat down and see if it decides to follow us?"

Sally hesitated. "That won't prove anything."

"I know," Adam said, "but at least that way you'll get an idea if it has another master."

Sally reluctantly set the cat down. "All right. But if a big wolf comes along and eats it after we leave here I will hold you personally responsible, Adam."

"There are no wolves in Spooksville," Cindy said.

"Wait till the next full moon," Watch said. "Hike deep enough into the forest and you'll see a few of those nonexistent wolves turn into people."

"Let's get back," Adam said. "I need some ice cream."

They started back down the path. The cat took no time making its intentions clear. It followed them and Sally was delighted.

At least none of them had to carry it, Adam thought. He was worried about picking up any stray animal. It could have rabies, or worse.

Back in town they went to the Frozen Cow, the only ice-cream place in town, where only vanilla was served. Lately, though, they'd convinced the owner to put chocolate syrup on their ice cream so they could have a little variety. Each of them ordered a dish with two scoops and plenty of syrup. They had just sat down to eat when the cat jumped up on the table and tried to lick Cindy's dish. Before the animal could get to it, though, Cindy shoved it off the table.

"Hey!" Sally said. "Don't be so rough."

"An animal shouldn't be up on a table," Cindy said.

The cat didn't seem to agree.

Right then Cindy let out a howl of pain.

The cat had scratched Cindy's lower leg. Scratched it bad, Adam noticed. Cindy was already bleeding from four distinct lines. Cindy started to kick the cat away when Sally jumped up to stop her.

"You started it," Sally said. "You hurt it first."

"I didn't hurt it," Cindy protested. "I just pushed it out of the way."

"That's exactly what Hitler said about Poland at the start of World War Two," Watch remarked.

"I'm bleeding," Cindy went on. "And that cat is responsible. Get it out of here."

Sally reached down and picked up the cat. But not to get rid of it. "No," she said. "Animals have rights, too. I think you should apologize to the cat, Cindy."

Cindy snorted and picked up a white napkin to wipe her leg. "Like it would understand me," she snapped.

Sally scratched the top of the cat's head. "Cats are some of the smartest animals there are. They are descended from lions."

"And we all know how popular those are in Disney films," Watch remarked under his breath.

They returned to eating their ice cream, while Cindy simmered and Sally spoon-fed the cat half her dish. The cat enjoyed the vanilla ice cream, but not the chocolate syrup. When they were finished, Cindy angrily left to go home for a bandage. Watch and Adam followed Sally home. The cat was sticking close to Sally now, never moving more than a foot from her legs. Sally seemed to enjoy the attention.

"Can you believe that Cindy?" Sally said. "She is so insensitive. She could have broken the cat's neck shoving it like that."

"I suspect this cat could jump off a three-story building and not get hurt," Watch said.

"Cindy got a pretty nasty scratch," Adam said. "Cuts like that can be dangerous. I don't think you can blame Cindy for getting upset."

Sally was annoyed. "Why do you always take her side?"

"Maybe he does so because your side usually lands us in a situation where we almost get killed," Watch said.

"I don't always take her side," Adam replied. "I just think you act rashly sometimes, is all."

Sally snorted. "I am spontaneous, not rash. There's a difference."

About the Author

CHRISTOPHER PIKE is the author of more than forty teen thrillers, including the Thirst, Remember Me, and Chain Letter series. Pike currently lives in Santa Barbara, where it is rumored he never leaves his house. But he can be found online at ChristopherPikeBooks.com.